THE SKY IS FALLING
(Little Chicken Charlie)

Written by
JUSTIN MATOTT

Drawn by
JOHN WOODS JR.

SKOOB BOOKS

LONDON   FRANCE   UNDERPANTS

THE SKY IS FALLING
(LITTLE CHICKEN CHARLIE)

Text copyright© 2004 by Justin Matott
Illustrations copyright© 2004 by John Woods, Jr.
All rights reserved under International and
Pan-American Copyright Conventions.
No part of this publication may be reproduced
or transmitted in any form or by any means,
electronic or mechanical, including photocopy,
recording, or any information storage and
retrieval system, without permission in writing
from the publisher.
Requests for permission to make copies of
any part of the work should be mailed to:
Permissions Department,
SKOOB BOOKS, Box 261183 Littleton, CO 80163.
Library of Congress Cataloging-in-Publication Data
Little Chicken Charlie by Justin Matott;
illustrated by John Woods, Jr. – 1st ed. p. cm.
Summary: A fractured fairytale story of courage,
using new characters and those from days gone by.
ISBN 1-889191-05-1
{1. poetry. I. John Woods, Jr. 1954— ill. II. Title

First edition A B C D E   Printed in China

If you are interested in a school presentation or
more information about Justin Matott and his work please
go to www.author-illustr-source.com/justinmatott.htm
Please send email to John Woods Jr at
jdwoodsjr@comcast.net

TO: **M**E, **M**YSELF AND **I**
(**I** HAVE ALWAYS LOVED THE LETTER **I**!)
JM

TO: You, Yourself and Y
(I have always loved the letter Y!)
JW

ALSO, TO MY ONE TIME PERSONAL BULLY, **R**ONNIE,
FOR GIVING ME SO MUCH TO WRITE ABOUT.
PICK ON SOMEONE YOUR OWN SIZE NEXT TIME!
JM

A special thank you to Antelope Ridge, Castle Rock and Eldorado Elementary Schools for kind advice and enduring multiple drafts while I tried to get to something readable and mildly entertaining! A very special thank you goes to Mary Freeman, Judith Snyder and Wendy Jo Woody, three extraordinary educators for personal, professional and helpful feedback and friendship.

DISCLAIMER
IF YOU DON'T LIKE CHAOS AND A LACK OF ORGANIZATION, THIS BOOK MAY NOT BE FOR YOU!

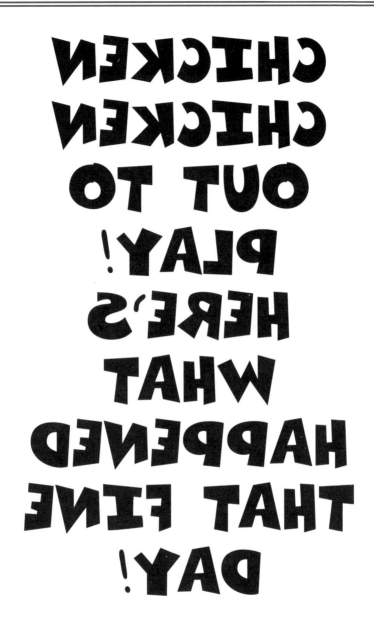

CHICKEN
CHICKEN
OUT TO
PLAY!
HERE'S
WHAT
HAPPENED
THAT FINE
DAY!

PLEASE HOLD THIS PAGE TO A MIRROR.

THE SKY IS FALLING
(Little Chicken Charlie)

WRITTEN BY
Justin Matott

Drawings by John Woods Jr.

Book design by Justin Matott

SKOOB BOOKS

London   France   Underpants

THE WUT PAGES

THE WUT PAGES
CONTINUED

Wut Xactly R U Looking 4?

~~ONCE UPON A TIME~~

(OH COME ON, THAT IS SO LAME! WHAT
KIND OF A WAY TO START
A STORY IS THAT?

AS MY FOURTH GRADE TEACHER ONCE
SAID,

"JUST JUMP RIGHT IN!
TELL THE TALE!"

NOW TRY AGAIN...

MAKE IT BIG,

MAKE IT **BOLD**,

MAKE IT YOURS!)

Hmmm... let's see, okay, try this...

It was a dark and stormy morn-

ing...

Is this going to be a scary story?

WHO SAID THAT?

Little Chicken Charlie stood in his garden as the sun peeked from behind a big, black cloud. Startled by his own shadow, he ducked down low.

WHOOSH WHOOSH

A gust of wind caused an apple to fall, clunking Little Chicken Charlie's head.

CLUNK CLUNK CLUNK

He jumped right out of his pants, running around like a chicken with his head cut off.

As the clouds dipped into his yard he **screeched**,

"THE SKY IS FALLING!

I MUST WARN THE MAYOR!"

<---NARRATOR ONE

Since he saw his shadow does that mean there would be more or less winter?

NARRATOR TWO--->

THAT'S PUNXSUTAWNEY PHIL,
A GROUNDHOG, NOT A CHICKEN,
YOU **DORK!** BESIDES, THIS STORY
TAKES PLACE IN THE SUMMER.
SHEESH!
AND ANOTHER THING, THIS IS
A FRACTURED FAIRYTALE; THE
GROUNDHOG DEAL IS A LEGEND,
A TOTALLY DIFFERENT THING!
NOW, JUST LISTEN TO THE STORY!

SHHH!

Dork? <---NARRATOR ONE

It's kind of weird that the narrators speak, but there are no quotation marks (the punctuation historically used to indicate speech). It seems to be in vogue today to go with or without. I guess Matott is trying to be a hip writer. Kids, don't try this in class.

Henpecked Harry gasped at the sight of a headless Charlie, but quickly realized his head had just disappeared into his turtleneck sweater.

whew!

"Little Chicken Charlie is such a coward!" Penny scowled, reclining on the couch, as she did every day, watching her soap operas while Harry worked. She wondered why Little Chicken Charlie was wearing a sweater in the summer.

"Well, he is a chicken dear," Harry replied meekly.

"Chickens aren't always *chicken* Harry! That's just an old wives' tale."

"You'd know. You're an old wife with a tail," Harry chuckled quietly.

"Bring me a cup of tea and a muffin!"

Penny groused.

(THE OLD BALL AND CHAIN ROUTINE!)

HOW ABOUT A PLEASE?

HEY,
WHAT ARE YOU
EXPECTING?

TEXT AND
PICTURES ON
EVERY PAGE?

HEAR

HERE

TWO?

TO?

TOO?

SHEESH!

Secretly spying
hungrily on
scared,
spineless
Little
Chicken
Charlie from
high in a tree,
the sneaky,
sharp,
sly, shifty,
shrewd
Foxy Loxy snarled;

"DRUMSTICKS! WINGS!
A BREAST! A THIGH!
I'LL CATCH THAT DUMB CLUCK,
'CUZ HE CAN'T FLY!"

A FOX IS A PREDATOR. A CHICKEN IS PREY.
LET'S PRAY THAT THE FOX DOESN'T GET
TOO PREDATORY ON THE PREY, EH?

First Narrator
- - ->

Is a chicken "chicken" like a scaredy cat?

Second Narrator
- - ->

A SCAREDY CAT? THERE ARE NO CATS IN THIS STORY. CHARLIE'S A CHICKEN, BUT HE'S AFRAID OF ALMOST EVERYTHING AND SOMETIMES WHEN YOU ARE AFRAID OF THINGS, PEOPLE CALL YOU A CHICKEN, SIMPLY MEANING YOU ARE SCARED.

First Narrator
<- - -

So are there brave chickens? Hey, did you notice that Matott is using quotation marks for the main characters and not us? Oh, and by the way smarty pants, look at page 44, THERE IS TOO A CAT IN THIS STORY!

Second Narrator
- - ->

SHHH...
JUST PAY ATTENTION TO THE STORY!

First ---> Narrator	KNOCK KNOCK
Second Narrator --->	**WHO'S THERE**?
First ---> Narrator	CHICKEN LITTLE
Second Narrator --->	**CHICKEN LITTLE WHO**?
First ---> Narrator	CHICKEN LITTLE, CHICKEN BIG, CHICKEN MEETS THREE LITTLE PIGS.
Second Narrator --->	**THAT IS A LAME JOKE**!
FIRST ---> Narrator	IT'S NOT A JOKE. READ ON...

OKAY, OKAY, YOU TWO, KNOCK IT OFF WITH THE KNOCK-KNOCK JOKES AND STORY INTERRUPTIONS! YOU ARE HERE TO CLARIFY AND ADD ANY MISSING ELEMENTS TO THE STORY. THIS IS NOT ABOUT YOU!

First Narrator: "Oops, sorry."

Second Narrator: "**I**T WON'T HAPPEN AGAIN."

First Narrator: "Think they'll fire us?"

Second Narrator: "**SHHHH**!
DON'T GIVE THEM ANY IDEAS."

First Narrator: "Hey, Matott started using quote marks for us..."

Second Narrator: "**S**TOP TALKING! **NOW**!"

We interrupt this story to bring clarification. So much is going on because the author has attention "issues" and can't seem to stay on subject.

Thus far in the actual story of Little Chicken Charlie, aside from all of the narrator intrusions, all that has happened, quite simply, is that Charlie has been bonked on the head and thinks the sky is falling. He and others will try to make it to the Mayor's house to alert the authorities.

Charlie's phone rang.

RING! RING!

He ran into his house. "Hello?"

It was Lucky Duck Laverne. "Hello Charlie. Walk with me in the woods?" she offered, hoping he'd propose marriage.

RING? RING?

Charlie yelled into the phone,

"I CAN'T STROLL
IN THE WOODS TODAY!
THE SKY IS FALLING!
I MUST WARN
THE MAYOR!"

"I'LL MEET YOU ON THE WAY!"

(Laverne peered out at the growing storm.)

Charlie ran out his front door.

ZZZZZOOOOOOOOMMMMMMM

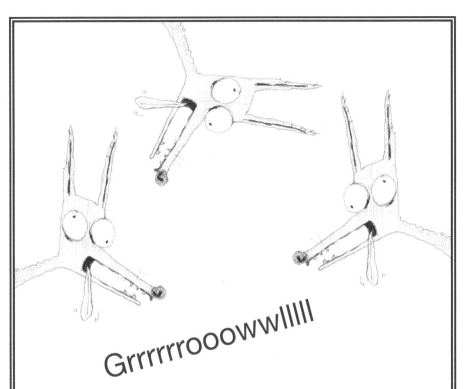

Grrrrrrooowwlllll

Foxy Loxy's
stomach turned and growled.
She sneaked into the shadows,

"Battered chicken!
Dumplings too!
I'll eat that chicken!
That's what I'll do!"

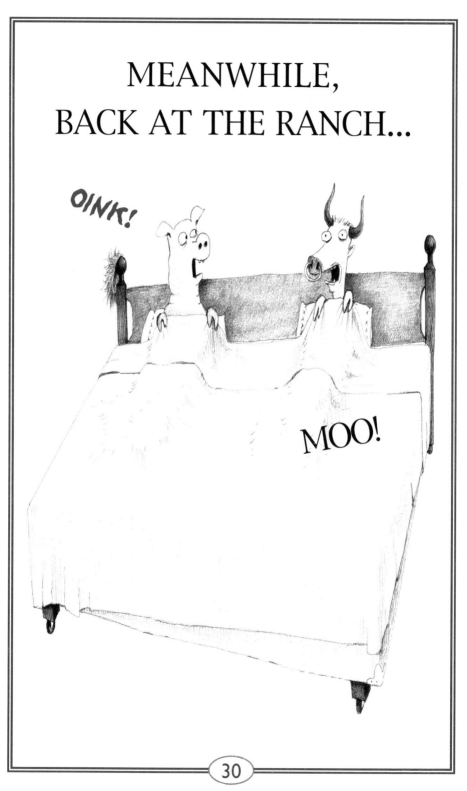

Laverne's been in love with Charlie ever since a kindergarten finger-painting class. They had been put together because neither of them had fingers.

<---First Narrator

SO THEY HAD A FEATHER PAINTING CLASS INSTEAD?

<---Second Narrator

Something like that.

<---First Narrator

YOU ARE A VERY, VERY STRANGE MAN, NOW S**HHH**... JUST PAY ATTENTION TO THE STORY!

<---Second Narrator

Do you think maybe Laverne is actually the Ugly Duckling and that whole thing about her really being a swan in the end is a fake?

First Narrator
--->

Second Narrator
<---

NOW THAT ISN'T VERY NICE!

Harry yelled as loud as he could from his window,

"CHARLIE, WHY ARE YOU SO UPSET?"

NAG, NAG, NAG!

NAG, NAG, NAG!

Penny popped a candy into her mouth, and nagged on... "Harry, you've windows to wash! Floors to sweep! The garden needs tending! You don't have time to talk to that chicken!"

Charlie yelled, "HARRY, DID YOU HEAR ME?"

"THE SKY IS FALLING! WE MUST WARN THE MAYOR!"

JEEZ, TALK ABOUT THE CHICKEN THAT ROARED!

DIDN'T YOU ALREADY SAY THAT?

WHO SAID THAT?

Surprised by Charlie's outburst, Penny whispered,
"I've never heard Charlie
raise his voice before."

"Good for you, Charlie!" Harry muttered,
feeling braver himself, he grabbed Penny's hand
and sprinted after Charlie.

Laverne met them by the town bridge.
Charlie yelled, "THE SKY IS FALLING!
WE MUST WARN THE MAYOR!"

Q. Why does Charlie keep saying the same thing over and over?
A. Because repetition is good for the younger readers.

From beneath the bridge growled a gruff voice:

"TRIP! TRAP! TRIP! TRAP! WHO'S THAT TRIPPING OVER MY BRIDGE?"

First Narrator: How romantic, a chance meeting between Charlie and Laverne...

Second Narrator: **THERE'S NOTHING CHANCE ABOUT IT!** REMEMBER THE PHONE CALL?

First Narrator: Huh?

Second Narrator: **PAY ATTENTION**!

First Narrator: I bet this turns into a kissy-kissy story!

Second Narrator: **YUCK! NOW SHHH**... YOU'RE GROSSING THE CHILDREN OUT.

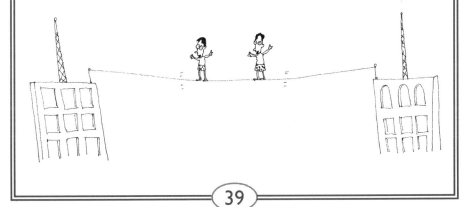

Charlie puffed himself up and yelled,

"LOOK TROLL, THERE'S NO TIME FOR YOUR BULLYING! THE SKY IS FALLING! WE MUST WARN THE MAYOR! LET US PASS! NOW!"

Penny whispered, "That's the second time Charlie's stood up for himself today!"

AHHH, MY HERO!

Laverne looked at Charlie admiringly.

Suddenly, the terrible Troll popped up sheepishly. **"May I come along?"**

ROAR?

Three Billy Goats Gruff followed, eyeing Troll nervously, feeling bolder seeing

Charlie take con trol.

They all ran toward the
Mayor's house, yelling,

"THE *SKY* IS **FALLING!** ꙍꬲ MUST **WARN** THE *MAYOR!*"

First Narrator: Wow, I thought that Troll was going to pluck that chicken.

Second Narrator: **BULLIES USUALLY BACK DOWN WHEN THEY ARE CONFRONTED!**

First Narrator: I knew that, but...

Second Narrator: **SHHH...**

Just then the Gingerbread Man (chased by an old woman, an old man and a line of hungry beings) collided with Charlie's group.

"RUN! RUN! AS FAST AS YOU CAN! YOU CAN'T CATCH ME, I'M THE GINGERBREAD MAN!"

Charlie shouted,

"GET YOUR OWN FAIRY TALE! WE WERE HERE FIRST!"

The Gingerbread Man stammered, **"But, I heard you were just a big chicken. Uh, may we help warn the Mayor?"** He looked nervously at the hungry mob.

Charlie glared, "LINE UP IN BACK!
DON'T TRY TO STEAL THE SHOW
WITH THAT RUN, RUN TALK!
LET'S GO!"

The growing group yelled,

"THE SKY'S
FALLING! WE
MUST WARN THE
MAYOR!"

First Narrator: Everyone's impressed with Charlie's sudden bravery!

Second Narrator: **HE'S** REALLY JUST WINGING IT!

First Narrator: Winging it?

Second Narrator: **G**ET IT? **IT'S** A CHICKEN JOKE, WINGING IT, MAKING IT UP AS HE GOES... **O**H, FORGET IT. **SHHH**...

First Narrator: Hey, no jokes from you! *I'm* the color commentator! By the way, did you know that bolding a character's name the first time it appears in a story is a screenplay technique?

Second Narrator: **WOW**! **M**ORE **U**SELESS INFORMATION!

47

Meanwhile, Foxy Loxy crept home to get ready for dinner with The Big Bad Wolf.

TIP-TOE TIP-TOE

"CHICKEN SOUNDS GOOD
FOR DINNER.
OR A NICE DUCK SALAD,
THAT MIGHT BE A WINNER."

Charlie and the growing gathering started up a crooked cobble-stone road. Across the street a boy cried,

"WOLF!"

as his red-hooded friend hid behind a tree.

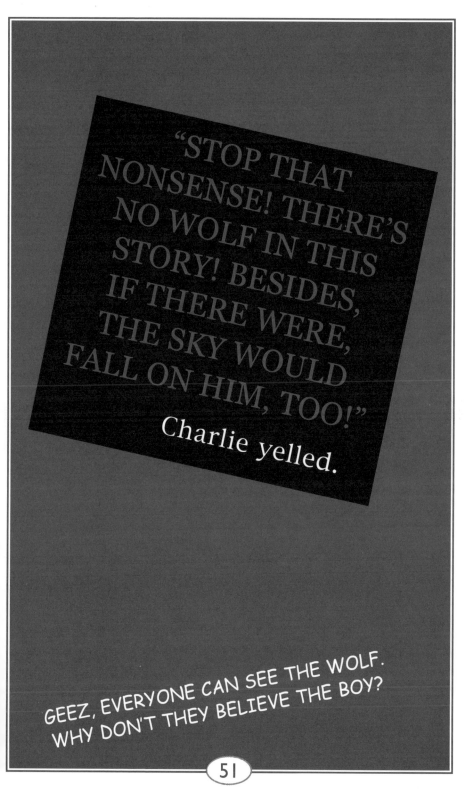

"STOP THAT NONSENSE! THERE'S NO WOLF IN THIS STORY! BESIDES, IF THERE WERE, THE SKY WOULD FALL ON HIM, TOO!" Charlie yelled.

GEEZ, EVERYONE CAN SEE THE WOLF. WHY DON'T THEY BELIEVE THE BOY?

First Narrator: Why did the chicken cross the crooked road?

Second Narrator: **W**HAT?

First Narrator: Get it, a chicken joke?
I crack myself up, like an egg, crack myself up! Get it?

Second Narrator: **WHY ARE YOU SO ANNOYING**? **Y**OU ARE CRACKED. **N**OW JUST BE QUIET AND LET ME WATCH THE ACTION. **SHHH**...

First Narrator: I AM THE COLOR COMMENTATOR. THIS IS WHAT I AM SUPPOSED TO DO.

Second Narrator: **WELL, I AM STARTING TO SEE RED. IS THAT ONE OF YOUR COLORS**?

CRACK JOKES? COME ON! GIVE ME A BREAK...

From behind a building strolled the
Big Bad Wolf dressed like a grandma,
talking QUITE LOUDLY on his cell
phone to his agent about his last role
in the Broadway production of Peter
and the Wolf.

The boy pointed and cried,
"WOLF! THERE!"

The Big Bad Wolf yelled into his phone. **"YOU HAVE TO GET ME BETTER ROLES!**

CRUNCH!

MUNCH!

CRUNCH!

I'M ALWAYS THE GUY WHO EATS PIGS, SCARES BOYS AND LITTLE GIRLS IN RED! I'M A *VEGETARIAN!* WHY AM I ALWAYS THE VILLAIN? CAN'T I EVER BE THE PRINCE? AND DO SOMETHING ABOUT MY WARDROBE! I AM DRESSED LIKE A GRANDMA FOR GOODNESS SAKE! WHAT WILL THE BOYS DOWN AT THE ELKS CLUB SAY?"

Everyone gasped.

"EAT US?"

The Three Little Pigs screamed
in unison.

"THAT'S NOT IN OUR SCRIPT!"

First Narrator: This new development with the wolf is interesting. He usually gets only one kind of role. (That is called typecasting, another Hollywood term. Hey, come to think of it, this story would make a great movie...)

Second Narrator: **SHHH!**
SHHH!
SHHH!

"A *vegetarian*?" Red Riding Hood gasped. **"How will children ever be afraid of the Big Bad Wolf again if he goes around screaming that he's a vegetarian? All suspense and drama are gone! I simply cannot work under these conditions."**

"Isn't a vegetarian an animal doctor?" one of the pigs asked.

Everyone rolled their eyes and turned back to Charlie.

You would think of all people, a pig would know that an animal doctor is called a veterinarian not a vegetarian!

Charlie yelled, "STOP IT, ALL OF YOU! I'M THE MAIN CHARACTER HERE! YOU'RE ALL LIVING IN A FAIRYTALE WORLD! NOW, LET'S GET BACK TO REALITY! **THE SKY IS FALLING!** WE MUST WARN THE MAYOR! NOW, STOP INTERRUPTING ME!"

Murmurs rolled through the crowd about Charlie's new boldness.

They all yelled
with him...

Standing at a lemonade stand in his yard, Foxy Loxy worked on his plan,

"FREE LEMONADE!
STEP RIGHT UP!
GET SOME COLD,
COME GRAB A CUP!"

Charlie and the parade passed by,

"COME ON! WE ARE NOT THAT DUM!" Charlie snarled.

How dum_b are you?

Foxy Loxy grew angrier, spying on the growing crowd. He'd heard the spreading rumors about the wolf's vegetarian ways.

"NOW I'LL HAVE TO GET A VEGGIE. I'M GONNA GIVE THAT WOLF A WEDGIE!"

First Narrator: So, which came first, the chicken or the egg?

Second Narrator: **W**HAT?

First Narrator: It's a philosophical question. Get it? One of them had to come first, but which?

Second Narrator: **Y**OU'RE VERY STRANGE. **Y**OU ARE SUPPOSED TO BE ADDING TO THE STORY, BUT YOU ARE REALLY JUST ALL ABOUT DISTRACTION. **N**OW **SHHH**!

Down the road, Charlie's auntie, Little Red Hen, stood in her farmyard with her lazy friends.

"Who will help me plant this wheat?" she asked.

"Not I," said the Goose.
"Not I," said the Duck.
"Not I," said the Dog.

Charlie yelled,

"AUNTIE RED HEN! THE SKY IS FALLING! WE MUST WARN THE MAYOR!"

She dropped her wheat seeds, and followed him. Behind her were a lazy goose, duck and dog.

**AUTHOR
OUT TO LUNCH!**

COME BACK LATER...

WOW! ARE YOU STILL HERE?
ISN'T THERE A BETTER BOOK
YOU COULD BE READING?

Foxy Loxy crept in the shadows, determined
to bring something home for his feast.
Charlie was standing in front of a mansion
preparing to tell the Mayor that the sky
was falling when Foxy Loxy pounced on him.

Charlie kicked Foxy Loxy
with all of his might, into
the clouds, where she landed
at the top of the beanstalk,
in front of a castle.

PICTURE
THIS SCENE IN YOUR MIND.
WE CANNOT SHOW THIS ILLUSTRATION.
THIS BOOK IS RATED "FF" FOR FAMILY
FRIENDLY. SUCH VIOLENCE CAN NOT
BE SHOWN IN THIS BARBARIAN
FASHION.

"KICKED MY BOOTIE,
UP INTO THE CLOUDS.
I WAS GOING TO EAT HIM,
BUT I GOT KAPOWED!
HE WAS SCARED,
BUT NOW HE'S NOT,
I THINK IT'S COURAGE,
OLD CHARLIE'S GOT!"

The owner, a giant, sniffing around for
a kid named Jack, spotted Foxy Loxy.
He carried her into the castle and put her in
a cage where his gold-egg-laying
goose had once been.

Meanwhile back on earth,
the crowd yelled,

"BRAVE **MAYOR!** THE SKY *IS* FALLING!"

First Narrator: Wow, so with a vegetarian wolf and the fox gone now, doesn't that lessen the tension too fast?

Second Narrator: **SHHH**...

First Narrator: Is that the same fox that eats the gingerbread man?

Second Narrator: **DON'T SPOIL IT FOR THE KIDS. SHHH**...

First Narrator: Note to author, The Little Red Hen story is technically a folk tale not a fairy tale.

Second Narrator: **YOU ARE REALLY GETTING ON MY NERVES!**

Meanwhile back at the Giant's castle the Giant was dressing Foxy Loxy up to look like Goldi-Loxy...

Goldi-Loxy? Oh, I can bearly, bearly, bearly stand it!
Three bearlys?
Get it?

The far-from-brave-mayor hid under his couch at the top of his mansion, having heard the commotion below. Though he was supposedly a big, tough rooster, inside he was just a chicken at heart. "I'M NOT COMING OUT!" he screamed like a kindergarten girl.

"Though I'm afraid of heights, I'll climb the wall to the Mayor's room,"

Charlie exclaimed boldly.

Next door, from her high tower,
Rapunzel let down her golden hair
so Charlie could climb onto the Mayor's
roof.

As Charlie started climbing, the air
was filled with a loud

RIIIIIPPPP...

Rapunzel's hair yanked off, sending
Charlie to the ground.
Everyone gasped, seeing Rapunzel's
shiny, bald head.

"She faked her way into my fairytale with a wig!"

a handsome frog prince screamed, as he stepped out of the shadows.

"Rapunzel, you tricked me! I should have auditioned for Snow White instead of this dumb story!"

The crowd booed.

"BOOOOOO!"

A wicked witch shrieked,

"OFF WITH HER HEAD!"

The nearsighted Wicked Witch missed and Rapunzel jumped onto a horse ridden by Rumpelstiltskin.

CLOP CLOP CLOP CLOP

GALLUP GALLUP GALLUP

They galloped away and would have ridden into a sunset if it hadn't been for the storm.

Charlie,
who had just gotten over
his fear of storms, bullies,
trolls, the falling sky, the
first ten drafts of this
story, wigs, Mondays,
storms, witches, the color
red, and wasting time,
looped Rapunzel's wig into
a lasso. He hurled the wig
lasso to the top of the
Mayor's mansion, swung
through the window
and carried the mayor
safely to the ground.

First Narrator: Well, it looks like everything is going to work out just fine...

Second Narrator: COME ON, WE STILL HAVE A LITTLE WAY TO GO. DON'T COUNT YOUR CHICKENS BEFORE THEY HATCH!

First Narrator: Count my chickens? Is the author going to add math? Get it, ADD math? Count?

Second Narrator: IT IS JUST A SAYING, MEANING... OH, WHY DO I WASTE MY BREATH? SHHH...

Everyone cheered together,

"HIP HIP HOORAY, CHICKEN *CHARLIE* **SAVED THE** *DAY!*"

"But dear Mayor, we thought you were brave. What happened?"

Mayor shrugged, "You can take the chicken out of the chicken coop, but you can't take the chicken coop out of the chicken."

Everyone tried to figure out what he meant, realizing he was using another saying wrongly, "You can take the boy out of the country, but you can't take the country out of the boy..."

Just then, the clouds lifted, the sun came out (the sky wasn't falling after all, it was just a low-lying meteorological disturbance), Rapunzel and Rumpelstiltskin looped back through town and rode into the sunset.

CLOP GALLUP

CLOP GALLUP

The last I heard, they were living happily ever after with their son Rumpelpunzel and their daughter, Rapstilzel and their dog, RumplePimple and their two cats, Zippy and Bob.

The Big Bad Wolf, tired of waiting for Foxy Loxy, decided to stroll downtown. As he entered the village, Little Red Riding Hood poked him in the chest, **"YOU should be ashamed of yourself dressed up to fool me like that!"**

A boy cried, **"WOLF!"**

No one believed him.

The big-vegetarian-polka-dot-boxer-wearing-not-so-bad-anymore-wolf
apologized.

First Narrator: Wow, this sure seems to be ending well. Courage is contagious.

Second Narrator:

Meanwhile everyone grew braver.

"From now on,
we share the chores!"

no-longer-Henpecked Harry scolded Penny boldly.

"The bridge is not just yours!
It's for public access! We'll cross
it if and when we want to! We're
not putting up with any bullies
ANYMORE!" the largest of Three Billy
Goats Gruff growled. Troll just nodded.
The smallest Billy Goat shouted

NO BULLIES!
NO BULLIES!
NO BULLIES!

YEAH!

Gingerbread Man stood on the mansion steps and announced;

"I won't run from you anymore, even if you can't catch me.
I have rights!
I WILL NOT BE EATEN!
I'LL SUE!"

Little Red Hen remarked to the duck, goose and dog,

"If you want some tasty bread, you'll help prepare it!"

Laverne took Charlie by the wing and whispered in his ear,

"Charlie, I've been in love with you for so long, but alas this isn't The Never Ending Story. I want to marry you, but I can't wait forever!"

Charlie said, "WHAT?"

"Charlie, I've been in love with you for so long, but alas this isn't The Never Ending Story. I want to marry you, but I can't wait forever!"

Charlie said, "WHAT?"

"Charlie, I've been in love with you for so long, but alas this isn't The Never Ending Story. I want to marry you, but I can't wait forever!"

Charlie said, "WHAT?"

"Charlie, I've been in love with you for so long, but alas this isn't The Never Ending Story. I want to marry you, but I can't wait forever!"

Charlie said, "WHAT?"

"Charlie, I said I've been in love with you for so long, but alas this isn't The Never Ending Story. I want to marry you, but I can't wait forever!"

Charlie said, "Oh, I thought that's what you said the first time!"

First Narrator: You'll stop shushing me for asking questions. If the author hasn't answered my questions, I've the right to ask!

Second Narrator looked at his contract, checking how many more books he had to work with First Narrator in.

First Narrator: Want to sign up for another assignment with me?

Second Narrator: **OH BROTHER***!*

First Narrator: JUST KIDDING. SHEESH.

Charlie dropped to his knee, "I'm no longer afraid. If I can weather the kind of storms I did today, marriage is not that scary. Will you marry me, Laverne?"

As it turned out, the Second Narrator was an ordained minister and performed the ceremony right then and there.

Everyone learned courage from Little Chicken Charlie that day.

The next year
Charlie ran for mayor and won.
To this day there's a bronze statue
in the town square with a
brass plaque honoring the new
and improved, braver, no longer
little, Chicken Charlie (just call him
The Honorable Mayor CHUCK!)

A BRAVR CHICKN
HAS NEVR
LIVED

A whisper came from the sky...

"FROM UP IN THE CLOUDS,
INSIDE THIS CASTLE
I WATCH THE ACTION BELOW
WHERE I CAN'T HASSLE...
I AM A FOX,
SO HUNGRY FOR CHICKEN
OH YES, I'LL BE BACK,
TO GIVE CHARLIE A LICKIN'!"

First Narrator: As they say in the movies, cartoons and in books, th-th-that's all folks.

Second Narrator: **SHHH,** WE'RE NOT QUITE DONE! READ YOUR SCRIPT!

Chicken Little is a folk tale from long ago about a little chicken that is hit on the head by an acorn and – believing that the sky is falling – goes to tell the king. He picks up friends along the way until they all run into the fox, who, in the original fairy tale, eats them all up.

The Gingerbread Man is a story of a lonely old couple, who, not having children of their own, create a gingerbread man, who, after being baked, jumps out of the oven and runs through the town and country taunting all with, "Run! Run as fast as you can, you can't catch me, I'm the gingerbread man!" In the end, a fox tricks the gingerbread man, the same way the fox tries to trick Chicken Little and his friends.

Rapunzel is a German tale of a husband and wife who are going to have a baby. They live next to a garden grown by a fairy where an herb called Rapunzel grows. The wife is sick so the husband steals some Rapunzel from the garden and feeds it to his wife. The fairy catches him and makes him agree to give her the baby, whom she locks in a tower.

The girl's hair grows long until one day a prince comes by and climbs her hair. And on it goes. There is no fox in this story

Three Billy Goats Gruff is about a troll living under a bridge who keeps the three goats from crossing the bridge to eat the sweet grass they desire. In the end the largest goat kicks the troll off the bridge, puts the bully in his place, and they cross to eat the grass. No foxes were used in this production.

The Little Red Hen is a story of four friends, three who are lazy, and one industrious and willing to do what it takes to get the job done. The theme is one about the value of good, hard work. The fox didn't get any of the wheat cake (bread) because he wasn't in this story.

JUSTIN MATOTT WOULD LIKE TO THANK ALL OF THOSE WHO CAME BEFORE HIM WITH THEIR ANIMAL TAILS, ER TALES, INCLUDED IN THIS FRACTURED FAIRYTALE. **A** BIG SPORTS FAN, ESPECIALLY **M**ONDAY **N**IGHT **F**OOTBALL, **M**ATOTT HAS ALWAYS ENJOYED THE WAY IT'S COMMENTED ON BY THE GUYS IN THE BOOTH LOOKING ON. **M**ATOTT THOUGHT IT WOULD BE FUN TO SEE THE **N**ARRATORS IN SIDEBAR CONVERSATIONS ASKING QUESTIONS AND TALKING ABOUT THE STORY AS IT PROGRESSED IN HIS BOOK ABOUT COURAGE.

"PSST... PASS THE SPORTS PAGE..."

JOHN WOODS JR. bravely works on books with Mr. Matott. He shows courage in his creations. He has illustrated other wonderful books that make much more sense!

Why did the chicken cross the road?
To get to the other side!

Why did the rooster cross the road?
To cockadoodle dooo something.

Why did the chicken cross the basketball court?
He heard the referee calling fowls!

Why did the turkey cross the road?
To prove he wasn't chicken.

Why did the chicken cross the road, roll in the mud and cross the road again?
Because he was a dirty double-crosser!

Why didn't the chicken skeleton cross the road?
Because he didn't have enough guts!

Why did the chicken cross the playground?
To get to the other slide!

Why did the horse cross the road?
Because the chicken needed a day off!

Why did the cow cross the road?
To get to the udder side!

Why did the chewing gum cross the road?
Because it was stuck to the chicken!

What do you call a rooster who wakes you up at the same time every morning?
An alarm cluck !

Why does a chicken coop have two doors?
Because if had four doors it would be a chicken sedan!

Why did the chicken end up in the soup?
Because it ran out of cluck !

It was a

dark and

stormy

morn-

ing!

WELL, THAT WASN'T A SCARY STORY AFTER ALL!

YOU'RE STILL HERE?

bok

bok

HEY! WHATCHA LOOKIN' AT?

THE END!

First Narrator:

WELL, THAT STORY WAS
FINGER LICKING...

Second Narrator: **STOP!**

YOU CAN'T SAY THAT!
THAT'S A TRADEMARKED AND
COPYRIGHTED PHRASE, WITH
ALL THE LEGAL PROTECTIONS
PROVIDED. SO, DON'T EVEN
THINK ABOUT SAYING IT.

First Narrator:

OKAY, WHATEVER YOU SAY. IT'S ALL

GOOD!

We hope you enjoyed our nonsense.

Come on bok, when you can stay awhile!

Be courageous!

So, did you get it?
It was a story about courage and being brave.
THE SKY ISN'T FALLING AFTER ALL!

OH, FORGET IT, WE'RE DONE. IF YOU
STILL DIDN'T GET IT, STILL DON'T
KNOW THE AUTHOR INTENDED TO
WRITE A HERO STORY, A STORY OF
COURAGE AND A STORY OF HEART,
THEN PLEASE GO BACK AND READ IT
AGAIN.

(By the way, next time you read this book,
you might want to skip the narrator jazz,
most of the odd numbered pages.
They are so annoying and it just
might make more sense!)

SEE YOU AROUND!

**NOT IF I CAN
HELP IT!**

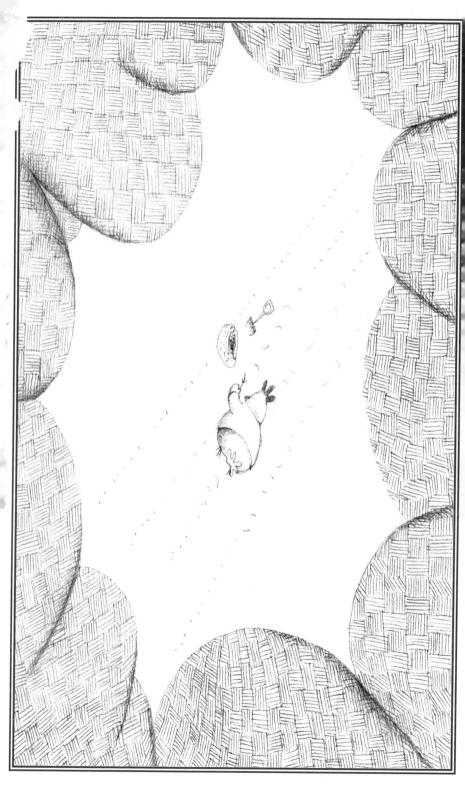

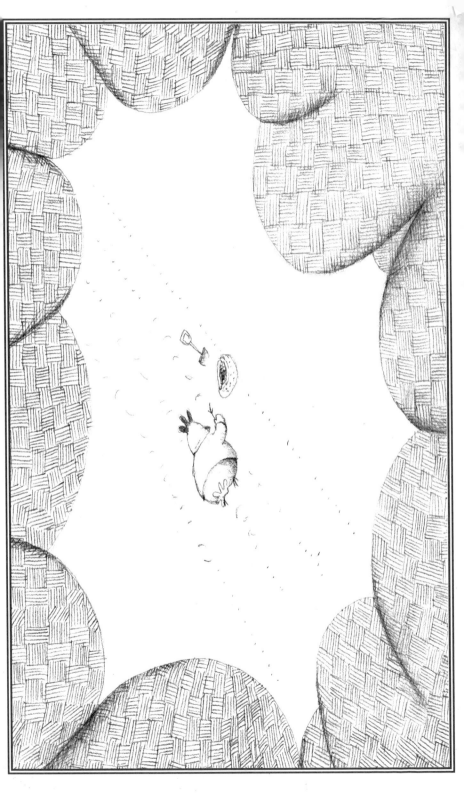